VELAKRO THE LIGHTNING BIRD

BY ADAM BLADE

With special thanks to Tabitha Jones

www.beastquest.co.uk

ORCHARD BOOKS

First published in Great Britain in 2022 by Hodder & Stoughton

1 3 5 7 9 10 8 6 4 2

A CIP catalogue record for this book is available from the British Library.

ISBN 978 1 40836 542 7

Printed in Great Britain

The paper and board used in this book are made from wood from responsible sources

Orchard Books
An imprint of Hachette Children's Group
Part of Hodder & Stoughton
Carmelite House, 50 Victoria Embankment, London EC4Y 0DZ

An Hachette UK Company
www.hachette.co.uk
www.hachettechildrens.co.uk

Welcome to the world of Beast Quest!

Tom was once an ordinary village boy, until he travelled to the City, met King Hugo and discovered his destiny. Now he is the Master of the Beasts, sworn to defend Avantia and its people against Evil. Tom draws on the might of the magical Golden Armour, and is protected by powerful tokens granted to him by the Good Beasts of Avantia. Together with his loyal companion Elenna, Tom is always ready to visit new lands and tackle the enemies of the realm.

While there's blood in his veins, Tom will never give up the Quest…

ORETON
PADDY FIELDS

TANGALA
PANIA
ARAN

There are special gold coins to collect in this book. You will earn one coin for every chapter you read.

Find out what to do with your coins at the end of the book.

You thought I was gone, did you not? Swallowed by the Netherworld, never to set foot in the upper world again... Consumed by the Beasts that roam this foul place... Well, it's not that easy to be rid of the most powerful magician who ever stalked the land.

I have the perfect plan up my sleeve, and soon I shall leave this Realm of Beasts behind.

And the best part? My arch enemy Tom will die in the process.

See you all very soon!

Malvel

THE FINAL BEAST

"What I wouldn't give for a warm fireplace and a bowl of soup right now," Elenna said, her teeth chattering against a driving wind that was cold and sharp as steel.

Tom stamped his feet as he trudged across the desolate black stone that stretched endlessly ahead, trying to get some feeling back into his numb toes. Kaptiva's forest lay far behind them. With night fallen, it was impossible to tell where the horizon became the sky.

"I would do anything to get out of this place, too," he said. "We only have one more candidate to rescue. Then we can leave the Netherworld for good." Tom hated to think of Rafe out here on his own. The boy from Tangala had grown up as an apprentice blacksmith, just like Tom, and Tom had felt an instant liking for the lad, with his mop of fair hair and shy manner.

We'll never let you win, Malvel, Tom thought, gritting his teeth. *We've saved Nolan, Katya and Miandra from your Evil Netherworld Beasts. And we'll save Rafe! Tangala will have its Master of the Beasts!*

Tom scanned for any sign of a landmark. There was nothing. He turned to Elenna. "Are we heading the right way?"

Elenna let out a heavy sigh and drew out the parchment Daltec had given them. The map had been made long ago by an eccentric wizard called Zarlo who had become trapped inside it. Before she unfurled the scroll, she raised an eyebrow towards Tom. "I still think it's odd that this found its way back to us."

Tom nodded, unease stirring in his gut. Zarlo's map had been snatched from his hand by an enchanted wind just before their battle with Kaptiva. In a stroke of luck that seemed almost too good to be true, Tom and Elenna had found the map on the ground after defeating the tree-Beast.

Before Tom could reply, a voice boomed from the parchment.

"Hello, friends! How wonderful that we are all together again."

"Don't you mean, why aren't we dead yet?" Elenna asked dryly. "That's normally your first question."

Zarlo chuckled. "I had my doubts that you'd survive the Netherworld initially, but you have proved my fears unfounded. Three Beasts defeated already! Extraordinary. I don't think you'll find the next one much of a challenge."

"What do you know of it?" Tom asked.

"Oh, she's barely a Beast at all," Zarlo said. "More an oversized bird, really. Her name is Velakro, and she's only a little bigger than an eagle. Defeating her should be a doddle!"

Leaning over the map, Tom spotted the small smudge of purple light that showed where the Beast was. It glowed close to a jagged coastline, still a long way off.

"We'd better get moving," he said, pacing onwards.

"What did you make of all that 'not much of a challenge' stuff?" Elenna asked once she'd put the scroll away.

"Well, I've never heard a Beast described as a doddle before," Tom said. "But at least Zarlo's sounding more cheerful."

"Hmm," Elenna said. "That's what I mean. He's not his usual grouchy self."

Tom nodded. "There's nothing we can do but keep going. Zarlo's our only hope of finding Rafe. But you're right. We should be on our guard."

Slowly, the sky lightened to the

heavy brooding purple of the Netherworld day. The barren rock beneath their feet began to slope upwards, gently at first, before getting rapidly steeper. Tom and Elenna were soon bent double with the effort of climbing into the wind. Gasping, his leg muscles burning, Tom focussed his mind on Rafe. *While there's blood in my veins I won't give up until we find you!*

Elenna suddenly stopped. "What is that noise?" At first Tom could only hear the howling of the wind, but then he made out another, deeper sound. A low, rhythmic whooshing accompanied by a hollow *boom*. He remembered the craggy coastline from Zarlo's map.

"We're near the sea," Tom said, a rush of adrenaline giving him new strength. "The next Beast isn't far." He loosened his sword in its scabbard and Elenna drew her bow from her back.

The slope levelled suddenly, and the rocky ground came to a jagged halt: a cliff. Tom and Elenna stepped to the edge and peered downwards.

Elenna gasped and recoiled from the plunging drop. Tom felt suddenly dizzy. Rugged shelves of glassy black rock fell away below them, each splattered with layers of green sludge. Even more alarming were the birds perched wing to wing on every ledge, their dark blue and red bodies pressed

close together. As Tom looked at their tiered ranks, they all turned at once to look up at him as if controlled by a single mind. Hundreds – no, thousands! – of glinting black eyes stared at Tom, filled with cold, alien hatred.

TREACHERY

"Janus birds," Elenna whispered, her face turning pale as she took another cautious look. She rubbed at the scabbed scratches that scored her forearms, caused by the flesh-rending talons of Janus birds when a flock had attacked her.

Tom took a deep breath as he ran his gaze over the rows of flinty eyes trained on him. At the base of the cliff, the blood-red sea sucked at a narrow crescent of sooty sand. The echoing *boom* of waves hitting the shore told of sea caves below.

"Do you think Rafe could be alive down there somewhere?" Elenna asked. "It sounds like there are passages weathered into the cliff."

"If he is, we'll find him!" Tom said. Suddenly, with a noise like a thunderclap, every Janus bird took flight. Elenna leapt back from the edge. Tom recoiled too, expecting an attack, but instead the birds wheeled around, soaring out over the red sea. Tom watched in horror as the creatures circled, drawing together to form a huge flock. The cloud of birds became denser, its edges sharpening, until Tom could make out the shape of a vast two-headed

bird. "Velakro! The Beast is formed from hundreds of Janus birds!"

Elenna shook her head in disgust. "A little bigger than an eagle… Isn't that what Zarlo said about the Beast? He was tricking us."

The giant creature had twin serrated beaks big enough to swallow Tom whole and gleaming red talons larger than any dragon's. The water below churned with the downdraft from the Beast's flapping wings.

"At least Zarlo led us to the right place," Tom said. "If the Beast is here, Rafe should be nearby. You go down and look for him, I'll keep our new friend busy."

"Remind me never to trust a wizard in a map again," said Elenna as she took one final look at the Beast, before lowering herself over the lip of the cliff.

Tom pulled out his sword. *Come on, then!* he taunted, using the power of the red jewel in his belt to speak straight into the Beast's mind. *What are you waiting for?*

Velakro's feathers glossed blue and red as she beat them in reply. Her blood-red talons were as sharp and deadly as scythes. Her twin pairs of eyes shone with a cold blue light. *You are almost too puny to trouble with, boy*, she said. Her voice grated like the screech of a rusty saw. *Nevertheless, I shall rid this land of you.*

The Beast dipped her heads and surged towards Tom. A mighty gust slammed into him, almost bowling him over as Velakro swiped for his face. Tom blocked with his sword, a rain of sparks showering down as he struck the giant talons. With a grating squawk, Velakro wheeled back, raking the cliff edge, sending chunks of rock clattering downwards. Down to where Tom knew Elenna must be!

"Elenna!" Tom shouted, his heart leaping into his mouth.

"I'm all right!" she called back, but Tom had no time to feel relief. Velakro shrieked with fury, then snapped one razor-edged beak at his throat. He smashed the bill away with the flat of his blade, but the Beast's other beak jabbed at his chest. Leaping back, Tom dodged the strike, then lunged, swinging his sword in a two-handed arc. It slashed through the feathers of Velakro's breast, slicing a deep cut, sending droplets of blood flying.

Velakro screamed, two harsh rasping cries filled with rage. She flapped her broad wings, climbing higher, well out of the reach of Tom's sword. As she glared down at Tom, her eyes flashed the silvery-blue of lightning. Energy began to crackle around her feet.

With a stab of fear, Tom reached for the shield on his back, but before he could wield it, twin beams of fizzing energy shot down from Velakro's talons.

Tom leapt back.

BANG!

The ground at his feet exploded,

catapulting him through the air and pelting him with sharp chips of stone. He scrambled up to see another sizzling jet already crackling towards him. Tom thought of Elenna, still climbing below. *I have to get the Beast away from the cliff edge.* He turned and ran.

CRACK!

Chunks of stone pummelled Tom's back.

BOOM!

Searing light filled his vision and the ground buckled, almost throwing him off balance as he hobbled on, bruised and breathless.

You can't outrun me! Velakro screeched. A fierce downdraft

buffeted Tom as the Beast flew overhead. She wheeled around to hover before him, her eyes blazing and her talons sizzling with deadly power. Tom skidded to a halt.

Trusting Ferno's dragon scale to absorb the deadly bolts, Tom lifted his shield as the Beast fired.

Bright golden energy slammed into Tom's shield, hurling him backwards as if he'd been kicked by a horse, though Ferno's scale had absorbed the worst of it. He landed hard on his back, the rocky ground punching the air from his lungs. Groaning with pain, Tom rolled over and staggered up. His shield arm was numb from the direct hit, and his head spun. An acrid, singed smell hung in the air. He realised it was coming from his own hair and clothes. Velakro had landed and was pacing towards him. Her eyes, no longer glowing, narrowed with spite. Glancing back, Tom saw he was almost at the cliff edge. *If Velakro fires again, I'm dead – and maybe Elenna too…* But the Beast's claws, like her eyes, had stopped glowing. In fact, her outline seemed to be fraying, as if she were coming apart. *Maybe she's run out of power!*

With a fresh burst of hopeful energy, Tom hunkered down and brandished his sword, ready to meet the Beast's attack.

Velakro stopped. Her outline was so ragged now Tom could see the individual Janus birds that made up her feathered wings.

Yield now! Tom told the Beast using the power of his red jewel. *Then I won't have to kill you!* The Beast dipped her head, and for an instant Tom thought she was offering her surrender. But then she let out a cold, mirthless cackle.

Can you fly? Velakro asked. Before Tom could form an answer, the Beast exploded into a screeching, swooping flock of Janus birds. They hit Tom like a tornado, their shrill voices deafening as he tried to keep his footing. Hundreds of wings battered Tom. Sharp beaks and claws jabbed and raked and slashed. Tom stumbled back, his stomach lurching as his heel overstepped the cliff edge… The birds kept coming, their wings beating against his chest and face. They screamed and pecked at his hair and clothes. He teetered, swiping at the creatures with his sword, but there were too many. His stomach flipped as, with a sudden rush of wind, the birds catapulted him backwards, right over the edge of the cliff.

SEA OF BLOOD

As Tom plummeted, he lifted his shield as high as he could, angling it to catch the wind. He felt a sudden jolt as Epos's magical eagle feather slowed his fall, tugging him out over the scarlet sea, but he was still going too fast…

SPLASH!

Tom hit the crimson sea feet-first

with a force that buckled his knees and jarred his spine. The water closed over him, salty and warm, as thick as syrup. A powerful current sucked him down. All sounds were muffled as red-tinged darkness pounded and squeezed Tom's body. He kicked his legs as hard as he could, forcing himself upwards, but he barely made any headway at all. Panic rising, Tom called on the magical strength of his golden breastplate. He pumped his legs and began to swim, using his shield to claw himself higher. Salt burned his eyes and nostrils. His lungs were screaming for air and his legs ached, but he thrashed towards the dim light above. Finally, his head broke the surface and he gasped, sucking in a huge breath. The heavy water clung to his sodden clothes, threatening to pull him back under. With stinging eyes, he could just make out the black cliff rising from the waves ahead and a narrow strip of inky sand. He blinked and saw Elenna, beckoning frantically.

"Tom!" she cried, just as his head went back under. Tom managed to surface again and kicked forwards, fighting through the nightmarish tug of the waves. Finally, his knees brushed the seabed. He tried to stand but didn't have the strength. Instead, he crawled, dragging himself through the shallows until he reached the sand and collapsed, gasping and exhausted, at Elenna's feet.

She helped him to stand up.

"I don't know what that stuff is," Tom said, between pants. "But it isn't like any seawater in Avantia. Where's Velakro?"

"She's vanished," Elenna said.

"She must have thought you were dead. There's no sign of Rafe either, but there are lots of caves. Maybe he's sheltering inside."

Tom nodded. "Let's go." The black sand of the beach was splattered with green droppings, but the Janus birds had gone. Shallow caves pockmarked the base of the cliffs and Tom and Elenna searched them in turn. Again and again, the only thing they found inside was wet sand, crusted with pink salt, and slimy droppings. Each cave was as dank and deserted as the last and a horrible salt and iron stench hung in the air, like a butcher's yard. The final cave they searched reached deeper into the rock face. Near the back, Tom spotted a murky red pool with something metallic glinting dully beneath the surface. As he

drew close, his heart sank. *A blacksmith's hammer*. Tom lifted it from the pool, the heft of it as familiar to his hand as his sword. It was well worn with use but still shiny. The rest of the cave was as empty as the others had been.

"Rafe's weapon," Elenna said. "But

what does it mean?"

Tom shook his head, remembering the hideous tug of the blood-red waves and the murderous glint of the Beast's cruel eyes. He tucked Rafe's hammer into his belt, heavy with dread. "Nothing good, I fear," he said. "But we can't give up. Not yet."

Stepping back out on to the beach, Tom cupped his hands to his mouth and shouted as loud as he could. "Rafe! It's Tom of Avantia! We've come to take you home!" Elenna joined her voice to his, and they both called until they were hoarse. No reply came. The only sound was the hiss of the waves.

Suddenly, a furious shriek pierced the quiet, echoing from above them.

"Velakro," Elenna said glancing up. "But I can't see her." Tom put his hand to the red jewel at his belt, frustration burning in his chest.

Show yourself! Tom cried.

Leave this place! Velakro answered, her voice like sandpaper rasping on stone. *Whatever is left of the boy you seek belongs to me!*

"The boy belongs to no one!" Tom shouted out loud. "What have you done to him?"

Elenna's eyes widened fearfully. "Listen," she said. Over the rush of waves, Tom heard a distant thrashing sound – the clap of a thousand wingbeats. And it was getting louder by the moment. He looked upwards to see a ragged black cloud pour over the cliff edge as the immense flock of Janus birds returned. Elenna hurriedly fitted an arrow to her bow. Tom lifted his sword. Already, the birds were gathering above them, drawing together to form the huge two-headed shape of Velakro. The Beast's four eyes began to glow with the silver-blue sheen of lightning.

"Run!" Tom told Elenna, just as the Beast sent a fizzing blast of energy towards the edge of the cliff, right over their heads.

CRACK!

Tom and Elenna raced away along the narrow beach as huge boulders thundered down the cliff, crashing onto the sand behind them.

I told you before, running is futile, Velakro cried. Tom glanced up to see her flying along the cliff edge, easily keeping pace with them. Her talons already sizzled with more energy.

BOOM! CRASH! BOOM!

Deadly avalanches tumbled down all around Tom and Elenna. The air was filled with choking dust and rocks of every size. A boulder slammed down right in front of Tom, almost crushing him. He darted around it, heart thumping, and spotted a cave ahead. He didn't want to risk getting trapped – but it was that or be pummelled to death.

"In here," Tom called to Elenna, ducking inside. She joined him, panting, her face grey with dust, and bleeding from new cuts. The thud of falling rocks quickly fell silent. Instead, Tom heard a high gleeful cackle.

You have nowhere left to run! Velakro crowed.

The pounding of blood in Tom's ears grew louder as hot, boiling rage built inside him. He gritted his teeth and yanked Rafe's heavy hammer from his belt. How dare such a powerful Beast stoop to harming an unarmed boy. *I won't run,* Tom told

Velakro through the power of his ruby jewel. *I mean to fight!*

Leaping back out into the open, Tom turned his gaze upwards. Four blazing silver eyes stared down at him. The Beast was hovering overhead, her clawed feet crackling with energy – but Tom didn't intend to wait for her to shoot first. Channelling his rage and his fear for Rafe, he called on the magical strength of his golden breastplate and drew back his arm, every muscle fibre welcoming the familiar weight and grip of the hammer. Then he let it fly. The hammer spun through the air faster even than one of Elenna's arrows. *THUD!* Rafe's weapon smashed square into one of Velakro's massive heads. The injured head dropped limply, hanging at an angle, the bright eyes turning milky and dull. A desperate grating scream tore from Velakro's remaining beak and her wingbeats faltered. Tom watched, his jaw set with grim satisfaction, as the Beast flapped out over the sea, tipped sideways, then plunged into the crimson waves.

She struggled briefly, thrashing her waterlogged wings but couldn't get any lift. A moment later, her head went under, and she sank from view.

"You did it!" Elenna said, emerging from the cave to stand at Tom's side. "You defeated Velakro."

Tom's shoulders slumped. All the savage fury had burned out of him, leaving him cold and tired. "Yes," he said. "But it means nothing if Rafe is gone."

THREATS AND PROMISES

Tom waded out into the shallows to retrieve Rafe's hammer. It might be the only thing left to return to the boy's grieving parents. When he got back to Elenna she was gazing out over the waves, her face drawn with sorrow.

"What now?" she asked. "Surely

there's some hope Rafe's still alive?"

"How can he be?" Tom asked, making a sweeping gesture at the rock face behind them. "We've searched all the caves. There's nowhere left for him to hide. But we can't let Malvel get away with this. He will pay for his crimes."

"I can think of another wizard with a debt to pay!" Elenna said grimly. She drew Zarlo's map from her tunic.

"Is it done?" Zarlo asked hurriedly as Elenna unrolled the parchment. "Are the pesky Avantians dead?" Once Elenna had the map fully opened, the wizard coughed and spluttered. "I mean... Ha! What I meant to say is, have you defeated Velakro, my dear friends?"

Elenna looked like she was going to rip the map in half. "Who did you think you would be talking to?"

"I was...just a bit muddled," Zarlo said. "It's not easy keeping track of what's going on when you're stuck inside a map." Tom could see Elenna's fingers turning white where she gripped the parchment.

"You lied to us!" Tom cried, his own hands shaking with fury. "Velakro was nothing like you said. She was huge. And terrifying!"

"How odd," Zarlo said. "I must have been mistaken. I—"

"Rubbish!" Elenna snapped, cutting

him off. "You knew. In fact, I think you're in league with Malvel. We can't trust a single word you say!"

"It's not like that," Zarlo whined. "Give me a chance to explain."

"You'd better be quick," Elenna said. "You have until the count of three to convince me I'm wrong. After that, I'm going to use your map for target practice."

"Please…

no! I'll tell you everything."

"One..." Elenna snapped.

Zarlo let out a terrified yelp. "All right, I admit it. It wasn't just good fortune you found my map when you did. Malvel planted it."

"I knew it!" Elenna said.

"Go on," Tom told Zarlo sternly.

"I just wanted to get out of this wretched prison!" Zarlo said. "Malvel promised me he would set me free using the *Book of Derthsin* if I lured you towards the next Beast. And... well...since that's where you wanted to go anyway, I didn't see the harm. I always knew you'd defeat the Beast."

"That's not true!" Tom cried. "You spoke a moment ago as if you hoped we were dead. You're as bad as Malvel. Worse, maybe – at least he doesn't pretend to be good."

"No. You've got it all wrong!" Zarlo insisted again. "I don't want anyone dead, but I've been trapped for longer than you can imagine. For the first time in centuries, I felt hope. I'm not evil. I'm just old and weary. I can still help you fight Malvel. Please don't destroy me. Please."

Tom closed his eyes and took a deep breath, trying to calm his temper.

"You're right," he said at last. "I can't imagine what it must be like to be trapped as you are. I can see it would drive you to desperate acts. But that doesn't mean we can trust you. Your treachery may have cost Rafe his life."

"Rafe's not dead!" Zarlo said. "I know where he is. I can show you. Just give me one more chance. I'll help you sneak into Malvel's lair. You'll find the boy there."

Hope squeezed Tom's heart like a fist. He desperately wanted to believe that Rafe was alive and well. He caught Elenna's gaze. He'd never seen her eyes blaze with such anger.

"What do you think?" he asked her.

She rolled up the map – not gently – so they could speak without Zarlo hearing.

"I don't think we can trust Zarlo as far as we can throw him," Elenna said. "But if there's any chance that Rafe is alive, we have to try and find him, even if that means walking into Malvel's trap."

A sudden blast of wind howled in off the sea. Tom turned to see high, foam-tipped waves forming in the distance. A small dark shape lifted from the water, droplets spilling from its wings as it took flight. A Janus bird. Tom frowned. Another bird emerged, then another. Touching the red jewel in his belt, Tom felt a burning shock of anger that wasn't his own. "The Beast isn't dead!" he told Elenna.

She unrolled Zarlo's scroll, and sure enough, Tom saw a weak purple dot pulsing over the ocean – getting steadily brighter.

"We should go before she recovers her strength," Elenna said. Then she glared down at Zarlo's map. "Lead us to Malvel. But if you lie to us again, I'll personally tear you into a thousand pieces and scatter you to the wind!"

Janus birds continued to lift from the stormy sea in twos and threes as Zarlo directed Tom and Elenna around the base of the cliff, following the narrow strip of black sand. Rolling waves powered towards them, throwing up salty spray and covering the beach with tattered clumps of pink foam.

A mist rose too. It was pink and cloying, leaving a slick film on Tom's skin, and it had the same rusty slaughterhouse tang as the caves. He and Elenna waded through knee-high breakers and clambered over rocky outcrops, narrowly avoiding patches of sucking quicksand. The hideous fog drifted in banks around them. With visibility so poor, Tom realised they would have to rely on Zarlo far more than they'd hoped. They needed a bargaining tool that would make sure the wizard remained loyal.

"I have a friend called Daltec who

is a powerful wizard," Tom told Zarlo. "If you keep your word, once we have Rafe safely back in Tangala, I'll ask Daltec to free you."

"Really?" Zarlo said, excitedly. "In that case, I'd definitely better make sure you don't die."

Tom and Elenna looked at each other and rolled their eyes, then forged onwards, following the rugged coast. Eventually, they rounded a jutting peninsula to find a craggy bay. They both stopped and stared.

"Very Malvel," Elenna said dryly. Even in the mist, there was no way to miss the Dark Wizard's fortress. It jutted from the cliff at the head

of the bay, shaped from the black rock itself. High towers with elaborately carved peaks and gables soared into the purple sky. Hideous gargoyles in the shapes of Beasts crouched above every casement and jagged finials as sharp as daggers topped the pointed roofs.

"How can he have built all that by

himself?" Elenna asked.

"The *Book of Derthsin*," Tom answered, a cold, clammy dread creeping over his skin. "It's so powerful he can create anything he wants. Or get his Beasts to do it for him. It won't be easy to get inside the fortress, that's for certain. Or out again..."

MALVEL'S FORTRESS

Tom and Elenna crouched together behind a ridge of stone, gazing out at the immense fortress. "How do we get in without being seen?" Elenna asked. Tom looked at the castle's huge door – surrounded by windows, there would be no way to sneak through it.

"That's where my particular knowledge and skills come in," Zarlo piped up from his map. "A network of old tunnels runs through these cliffs. Malvel built his castle right on top of them. At least one tunnel should come up beneath it."

Tom didn't like the idea of heading below ground with only Zarlo to guide them. But they didn't have much choice.

"Can you show us how to get in?" he asked.

The map suddenly started to glow with a soft yellow light. "See how helpful I am!" Zarlo said. "You'll find the entrance to your right."

Tom and Elenna kept low to the

ground as they skirted the rock face, searching for the opening. They soon came across a weathered, almost circular cavemouth, partly hidden by a rockfall.

It was wide enough for Tom and Elenna to stoop and enter side by side.

The dim glow of Zarlo's map illuminated smooth, damp walls

covered in reddish slime. The air was stuffy and uncomfortably warm. More gunk hung from the ceiling and Tom had to hunch over to avoid the long, dripping strands, like blood-tinged mucus. As they travelled deeper into the cliffs, Tom couldn't shake the feeling that he was inside the gut of some gigantic Beast.

"This cave doesn't look natural," Elenna said. "The walls are too smooth. And look..." She pointed to a set of parallel gouges scored in the rock face. "There are tool marks under the slime."

"Not tool marks," Zarlo said. "They're tooth marks. The

Netherworld is home to Beasts so terrible you couldn't even imagine. If they were ever to get out into the human world, nothing would stand in their way."

"You forget I am Master of the Beasts," Tom told the wizard sharply. "I've fought Beasts you couldn't even imagine. Elenna and I would stand in their way. And I hope Malvel hasn't given you any ideas."

"No, no. Of course not!" Zarlo said. "I was merely providing information."

Despite what he'd told Zarlo, the idea of meeting a Beast in such close quarters made Tom's body fizz with nerves. He kept one hand on the hilt of his sword as they pressed further into the dark.

The tunnel twisted and turned, branching often, like the roots of a tree. Each time they reached a fork, Zarlo directed them without hesitation. They made so many turns that even with the enhanced memory of his yellow jewel, Tom wasn't sure he'd be able to find the way back out. They walked in silence, listening for any movement ahead – any signs of Rafe or Malvel. But apart from their own muffled footsteps, the only sound was the constant drip of slime on rock. Drops rained down on Tom too, making his skin crawl. Elenna was constantly dashing the stuff from her face and wiping Zarlo's map with her sleeve, but it was no use – they were all soon covered. Elenna let out a small cry and drew back from a mangy clump of matted feathers on the ground.

"A Janus bird," she said, stepping gingerly around it. "It must have got lost in here..."

Tom shuddered. The thought of perishing in this labyrinth, without even the dim light of Zarlo's map was too horrible.

The tunnel went on and on. Tom's neck ached from constant stooping and his damp clothes chafed his skin. He longed for the taste of cool air and the chance to stretch his stiff muscles. Then suddenly, without warning, his wish was granted. The tunnel widened and began to climb. A fresh breeze stirred on Tom's skin.

"Almost there," Zarlo told them.

"We'd better be ready to fight," Tom said, flexing his shoulders and drawing his sword. He offered Rafe's hammer to Elenna. "It's too small in here for your bow." Elenna took the weapon and tucked it into her belt, keeping her hands free for Zarlo's map.

The tunnel continued to climb sharply, then levelled, opening into a huge cavern. In the wider space, Zarlo's map barely lit the way three paces ahead, but Tom could see what looked like tall archways on either side. He heard a soft shuffling sound from ahead and stopped dead. Stealthy footsteps.

From the look in Elenna's wide, watchful eyes, Tom knew she'd heard it too.

"Wait here," he whispered, then crept forwards, raising his sword. His skin prickled with anticipation as he stole onwards, more than ready to meet his oldest enemy.

Suddenly, a figure leapt from the darkness and barged into him, barrelling him sideways. Tom tumbled through an arch and down a flight of sharp stone steps.

His attacker fell too, landing heavily on top of him. Strong hands closed around Tom's throat.

Gasping and choking, Tom grabbed a fistful of his attacker's clothing and rolled, forcing his adversary beneath him, then he thrust a knee downwards into his opponent's gut. With a grunt, Tom's attacker loosened his grip. Tom yanked his sword arm free and drew back his blade.

"Tom!" Elenna called, arriving in a clatter of footsteps. The glow of Zarlo's map lit the scene. Now that he was finally able to see his attacker's face, Tom lowered his sword. A pair of wary, haunted blue

eyes stared up at him from beneath a shock of blond hair.

"Rafe!"

THE ARENA OF BEASTS

As Tom heaved himself off Rafe, the boy struggled to his feet, clutching his stomach.

"Tom of Avantia?" Rafe wheezed. He was stocky, with broad muscular shoulders, but thinner than Tom remembered. Rafe's freckled skin was covered in scratches and grime, and his tunic was badly singed.

Tom nodded, guilt tainting his relief. "I'm sorry I hurt you," he said. "We've come to send you home."

"How did you get here?" Elenna asked. "Did Malvel capture you?"

"Malvel?" Rafe asked, with a puzzled frown. "I haven't seen anyone since I arrived here – only birds. One moment I was fighting in the trials, and the next thing I knew the ground opened up and I was drowning in a sea of red jelly. I managed to get out and on to a beach, but everything was the wrong colour. I thought at first I must be dreaming, or dead..."

"No," Elenna said. "This place is

real. You were transported to the Netherworld." She offered Rafe her water flask. He took it and drank deeply.

"Thank you," the boy said, his voice stronger.

"How did you end up in these tunnels?" Tom asked.

Rafe looked down at his feet. "A huge bird-Beast with two heads attacked me," he said. "She kept firing lightning from her feet. I tried to fight back, but she stayed too far away for me to use my hammer, and then a bunch of smaller birds attacked too. They snatched my hammer from my hand." A deep blush spread up the boy's cheeks as he went on. "In the end, I took shelter in these caves, but it was so dark inside I couldn't find a way out. I wasn't very heroic. If this was part of the trials, I have failed."

Tom put a hand on the boy's shoulder. "You didn't fail," he said. "This was never part of the trials. You did well to survive an encounter with Velakro."

Rafe looked up, brightening. "So, this is the real thing?" he asked. "A real Beast Quest?"

Tom nodded. "Malvel kidnapped you and the other candidates."

"But...isn't Malvel dead?" Rafe asked. "My father used to tell me stories about your Quests. He said you defeated Malvel."

"It seems Malvel is very hard to kill," Tom said. "But this time, he won't get away. Elenna and I are going to look for him after we've sent you home."

"We found this," Elenna said, handing Rafe his hammer.

"Thank you!" he said. "I thought it was gone for good."

Tom took the purple gem from his belt. "This jewel will open a portal," he told Rafe. "It will take you back to the palace in Tangala." Tom began to sketch a rectangle in the air, but instead of glowing brightly, his purple jewel gave a faint pulse of light, then went dark. Tom growled in frustration. "It's not working. Malvel's magic must be blocking my powers."

Rafe bowed his head. "Then at least I have a chance to show my worth. I will help you in any way that I can."

They climbed back up the stone staircase and continued along the hallway. Eventually, Tom made out a dim purple light streaming through an archway ahead.

Elenna put Zarlo's map away and

drew her bow from her back. Tom lifted his sword and, taking the lead, Rafe brandished his huge hammer.

As Tom stepped through the archway and out under the purple sky, he found himself in an immense, open-roofed arena. Massive pedestals ran along the walls, each topped with a life-sized statue of a Beast. Tom spotted dragons and serpents, gorgons and centaurs as well as other monsters he couldn't name. At the far end of the arena, seated on an intricately carved throne on top of a high dais, sat Malvel.

The Evil Wizard smiled. One

gloved hand rested lightly on the arm of his throne and in the other, he held a staff. His black hood was thrown back to show his gnarled, vulture-like features and his eyes burned with a feverish light.

"Welcome to my home," Malvel

said. "It took you far too long to get here, but I am glad you have finally made it. Now, if you could just hand over your purple jewel, I may even let you out alive."

Tom drew back his shoulders and lifted his head, staring Malvel in the eyes. "You know I can't do that," Tom said.

His smile turning as rigid as a skull's, Malvel let out a sigh. "So be it," he said. Then he clapped his hands.

With a rush of wingbeats, Velakro appeared. She landed on the mantel of a high archway behind Malvel, gripping the stone with her scarlet claws. Her injured head had partly recovered. It no longer hung down, but one of the Beast's eyes was swollen shut. With her three remaining eyes, Velakro glared at Tom.

Now you will die! she hissed in Tom's mind.

1

VELAKRO'S LAST STAND

Malvel clapped his hands again, and Velakro swooped from her perch, casting a vast shadow over the arena. Tom heard the *twang* of Elenna's bow as she quickly fired. Her arrow sliced through one of the Beast's wings – but it only dislodged a single Janus bird, which fell away with an angry *squawk*.

Velakro landed in the centre of the walled atrium. With her broad wings spread wide and her twin heads lifted proudly, she towered over Tom. Her red talons, as sharp as butcher's hooks, crackled with golden energy, and her three good eyes blazed so brightly they seemed to burn into Tom's soul.

Tom charged, sword raised high, just as the Beast lifted one huge foot and sent a blast of energy through the air. It fizzed past Tom, and a terrific *CRASH!* rang out from behind him, followed by a cry from Rafe. Glancing over his shoulder, Tom saw the boy on the ground, half covered by the rubble of a fallen statue. But with Velakro almost on him, Tom could do nothing to help.

Velakro's serrated jaws snapped towards Tom's throat. He lashed out with his sword, smashing them away, but her second, injured beak

jabbed for his gut. Tom ducked out of range, just as the Beast raised her foot and fired a deadly bolt towards him. Calling on the power of his golden breastplate, Tom braced himself against the impact and caught the beam with his shield.

SMACK!

Even with his magical strength, he was cannoned backwards, the heat of the blast singeing his skin. He crashed into a pillar and slid to the ground, winded and bruised.

Velakro flapped in close, craning over Tom, the tips of her claws barely a handspan from his feet. With his ribs on fire and his head spinning, Tom couldn't rise.

Fry! Velakro squawked, her eyes sparking.

Fear jolted through Tom. *This is the end!* But as the Beast raised her clawed foot, one of Elenna's arrows whizzed through the air and thudded into her flank.

Velakro screeched, the light in her eyes dimming a fraction. Tom hauled himself up, staggering woozily. *BOOF!* Pain exploded inside his skull as one of Velakro's huge beaks cracked down on his head, slamming him to the ground face down. Half-blinded with agony, Tom pushed himself up to kneeling, then felt something snag his belt – Velakro's beak! It yanked him into the air.

Velakro thrashed her head from side to side, jerking Tom about like a rag, rattling his bones. It was all Tom could do to keep hold of his sword and shield as he was tossed around.

"Let him go!" Elenna screamed. Through Tom's juddering vision, he saw her ready another arrow.

Velakro hissed with fury. *As you wish...* Tom's stomach lurched as the Beast tossed her head, flipping him into the air. Higher and higher he climbed – then he started to fall. As he plummeted, Velakro's beak opened wide beneath him – so wide he could see right into her gaping red throat. *She'll swallow me!*

Tom cast a panicked glance at Elenna. His friend was frowning and had an arrow aimed almost straight towards him. *Don't miss!*

THUD!

The arrow smashed into Velakro's beak, knocking it aside just in time.

Tom hurtled on towards the ground.

SMASH!

His arms buckled beneath him as he landed, and his cheek cracked against cold stone. From his dais, Malvel laughed with glee.

Tom somehow managed to push himself up on to his knees. Velakro was glaring at Elenna, her wicked eyes burning brighter than ever.

"Look out!" Tom shouted to his friend. Elenna leapt towards a statue, clearly hoping to take shelter behind it, but quicker still, Velakro sent another energy bolt flying. The blast hit the sculpture.

CRASH!

Shattered stone filled the air as the top half of the statue exploded. A fist-sized chunk hit Elenna on the temple. She dropped to the ground, eyes closed. On the other side of the arena, Rafe was struggling to free himself from the rubble that pinned him down. Looking from one to the other, Tom decided Elenna was in greatest need. He leapt to his feet and lunged towards her.

"Not so fast!" Malvel cried from his vantage point. The Dark Wizard lifted his staff, firing a red energy burst towards Tom. He dodged aside and raced on. Elenna's eyes fluttered open. She began to stir.

"Get the girl!" Malvel ordered Velakro, then aimed his staff straight at Elenna as she lay helpless on the ground. Tom called on the power of his golden boots and leapt towards his friend as Velakro flapped across the arena. He landed in front of Elenna and hunkered down, his shield and sword raised to defend her, but with a flick of one gigantic wing, Velakro swatted him aside. A shadow fell over Tom, and Velakro's scarlet claws slammed him to the ground, piercing his shoulder and chest, pinning him in place.

Do you have any final words? Velakro asked Tom, flexing her talons so that Tom winced with pain.

"Wait!" Malvel shouted. "Don't kill him. That will be my pleasure. I want him to see his dear friend Elenna perish first. Let him be and finish her." Tom felt a surge of frustration and anger from Velakro. But the Beast did as she was told, lifting her talons and setting Tom free. He leapt up. In the same moment, Malvel hurled a blast of blue fire towards him. It hit Tom with a crackle, like ice forming, freezing his muscles, locking him in place. He couldn't move. All he could do was watch in horror as Velakro crouched over his friend. Elenna let out a groan and opened her eyes. Seeing the Beast above her, she tried to rise but barely managed to lift her head before her eyes fluttered closed again.

Velakro's massive beak opened. She lowered her head towards Elenna. Tom called on every part of his magical golden armour at once and flexed all his muscles, trying to escape Malvel's power, but it was no use! He was utterly powerless.

A tremendous metallic *CLANG!* rang out, echoing all around the arena. Through a rising plume of dust, Tom could just make out Rafe standing beside the pedestal of a colossal statue, right behind Velakro. A wide crack ran through the full height of the stone Beast. Tom willed Rafe on. *You can do this!* The boy drew back his hammer again and slammed it into the damaged sculpture once more. *CRASH!* The statue burst apart, sending dust and debris flying, hiding Rafe and

Elenna from Tom's sight. As the air cleared, Tom saw that Velakro was no longer standing over his friend. Instead, the Beast was lying crushed beneath the ruins of the giant statue. One of her heads poked from the rubble, slack-beaked and misty-eyed. It showed no sign of life. Rafe stood blinking beside the now empty pedestal, covered in dust.

To Tom's relief, Elenna had escaped further injury. She opened her eyes once more and pushed herself up to a sitting position. Suddenly, Tom found himself able to move and he raced to his friend's side.

"Where's...Malvel?" Elenna croaked. Tom turned towards the

wizard's dais. The throne was empty.

"Looking for me?" a harsh voice called. Tom looked up to see Malvel flying in a chariot pulled by Janus birds. Under one arm he held the *Book of Derthsin*, and in his other hand he wielded his staff. A purple jewel set at the head of the staff began to glow – a jewel that hadn't been there moments before. *No! It can't be!* Tom felt for his belt. It was gone! *It must have come off when Velakro tossed me!*

"That's right!" Malvel crowed. "I've got what I came for. I wish you a long and unhappy stay in the Netherworld!" With a flourish of his staff, Malvel shot a beam of purple light into the air ahead of him. A wide portal opened, right in the wizard's path. Tom could see clear blue sky on the other side. *The sky of Tangala!*

"Goodbye!" Malvel called, and with a gleeful wave, he rode his chariot through.

AN EMPTY VICTORY

Tom watched in horror as the portal to Tangala vanished behind Malvel's chariot, leaving him staring at the heavy sky of the Netherworld. Elenna staggered to her feet. Rafe picked up a dusty object from the ground and held it out to Tom.

"Your belt," Rafe said, sombrely.

Tom took it and slowly, as if half asleep, fixed it around his waist. It hardly mattered what he did now.

Tom hung his head. "We've failed," he said. "And not only that, we're trapped." Elenna put a hand on his shoulder.

"We're all safe. That's the main thing. And we've defeated the Beast," she said. "Maybe Zarlo will know another way out of this realm. Or perhaps Daltec will find us."

"I hope so," Rafe said. "My father never really wanted me to come on this Quest. My family will be devastated without me."

"I'm so sorry, Rafe," Tom said. "We have you to thank for defeating the

Beast – but instead of a reward, you're trapped here. And all the while Malvel will be free to do as he chooses." Tom balled his fists. He had never felt so utterly defeated.

Elenna unrolled Zarlo's map. "Do you know of any portal back to our realm?" she asked the wizard. "We defeated the Beast, but Malvel stole Tom's purple jewel and escaped."

Zarlo made a sound like he was sucking in air through his teeth. "Oh dearie me," he said. "Do you want the good news first, or the bad?"

Elenna sighed. "Just tell us," she said.

"Well, the bad news is there's

definitely no other portal. I'm one hundred per cent certain of that. But the good news is you'll get to spend a lot more time with me! Oh, and the extra bad news, if you're interested, is that I don't think you've actually defeated the Beast."

Tom heard the clatter of stones from nearby. He turned with weary resignation to look at Velakro's buried corpse. It was gone. Instead, Janus birds were emerging from beneath the rubble. Lots of Janus birds.

Tom, Elenna and Rafe all stepped away from the shifting stones as hundreds of birds emerged. Tom's sword felt heavy and useless in his hand, but he lifted it anyway.

"We've defeated her once, we can defeat her again," Elenna said. But the Janus birds weren't forming a cloud or fusing together. Instead, each was finding a perch on the stone walls and statues surrounding Malvel's throne.

The birds began to twitter and squawk in a shrill discordant clamour. As Tom listened, he made out a voice in the jarring cacophony. Velakro's voice.

You have shown yourself to be brave and strong, Master of the Beasts, Velakro told him. *Now the wizard's gone, my fight is done. There will be no more killing.*

However, there is no place in this realm for your kind. You must leave.

One by one the Janus birds took flight and began to form a vertical circle in the air, swooping close to the ground before rising again. As more birds joined the strange dance, the space left in the middle of the ring shimmered with swirling purple and blue light.

"A portal!" Elenna said. "Zarlo – can you tell us where it goes?"

"I've no idea," the wizard said. "But wherever it leads has to be better than here. Hurry! Go through before it fades!"

Tom peered closely into the portal, but there was no clue in the shifting

colours as to what might lie beyond.

"Let's all go together," Elenna said. Tom wished he could be sure he was following Malvel. But he couldn't stay in the Netherworld. He nodded. "Ready?" Elenna asked Rafe. The boy cast an anxious glance at the portal, but quickly nodded too.

Tom, Rafe and Elenna all lined up side by side, and together they stepped through the portal.

Tom blinked in the sudden glare of sunlight, a bewildering rush of colour and noise flooding his senses. Looking around, he realised that they had arrived in the palace courtyard in Tangala, almost exactly where the candidates had originally disappeared. And judging from the throng all around them, it was market day.

"It's Tom! He's back!" a stout vendor shouted from a nearby market stall. "Elenna too! And isn't that young Rafe?" A clamour of voices went up and soon a chaotic press of bodies surrounded Tom, Elenna and Rafe.

"Make way!" an imperious voice demanded. The crowd parted, and Tom saw Prince Rotu striding through.

"Give them some space!" Daltec cried, hurrying closely behind the prince. A broad, muscular man with a bald head and thick red beard came next.

"My boy!" the big man exclaimed, tears swimming in his eyes as he rushed forward. An instant later, Rafe was folded in the giant's burly arms.

Tom felt strangely disconnected

from all the smiling faces and joyful shouts. Elenna suddenly gripped his arm. "It's Queen Aroha and King Hugo," she said. "Look!" The crowd draw apart once more, making way for the royal couple. Both Hugo and Aroha were grinning broadly, but Tom felt hollow and cold.

"Congratulations!" Hugo cried, clapping Tom on the shoulder, then Elenna. "I knew you would find them!"

"You both look like you need a good meal and a long rest!" Aroha said.

Tom dropped to his knees before his Queen and King and bowed his head.

"I'm afraid I have the most terrible news, your majesties," he said without rising. "There won't be time for us to rest. Malvel escaped. He has the *Book of Derthsin*, and I know him well enough to be sure he'll already be working his Evil. It is my fault he is free. But while there's blood in my veins, he won't be for long!"

THE END

CONGRATULATIONS, YOU HAVE COMPLETED THIS QUEST!

At the end of each chapter you were awarded a special gold coin. The QUEST in this book was worth an amazing 8 coins.

Look at the Beast Quest totem picture opposite to see how far you've come in your journey to become

MASTER OF THE BEASTS.

The more books you read, the more coins you will collect!

Do you want your own Beast Quest Totem?

1. Cut out and collect the coin below
2. Go to the Beast Quest website
3. Download and print out your totem
4. Add your coin to the totem

www.beastquest.co.uk

READ THE BOOKS, COLLECT THE COINS!

EARN COINS FOR EVERY CHAPTER YOU READ!

550+ COINS
MASTER OF THE BEASTS

410 COINS
HERO

350 COINS
WARRIOR

230 COINS
KNIGHT

180 COINS
SQUIRE

44 COINS
PAGE

8 COINS
APPRENTICE

550+
515
480
445
410
395
380
365
350
320
290
260
230
217
206
191
180
146
112
78
44
30
19
8

READ ALL THE BOOKS IN SERIES 28:

THE NETHERWORLD!

Don't miss the first exciting book in this Beast Quest series: OSSIRON THE FLESHLESS KILLER!

Read on for a sneak peek...

AN ILL WIND

A cloudless sky arched over Tangala's capital, Pania, and the sunlight glinted off the pointed spires of Queen Aroha's palace.

The day of the Trials had finally arrived and, judging by the packed benches all around him, Tom thought half of Tangala must have come to watch. He craned forward in his front-row seat between Elenna and Daltec, trying to get a better view of the contestants he and Elenna had helped select. The brave hopefuls waited in a fenced enclosure just off the main arena. Some were practising their moves, jabbing and thrusting their weapons. Others were limbering up or polishing their armour.

The contestants had travelled from all over Tangala to try out for the title of Master or Mistress of the Beasts. Men and women. Young and old. All willing to risk their lives to protect Tangala. Tom was pleased to see many of the applicants were young people. He and Elenna had insisted the contest should be open to all. After all, they knew better than anyone that heroes could come from humble beginnings.

Turning his attention to the tiered benches of spectators, Tom spotted cat-people from Viga sitting alongside fisherfolk and forest dwellers, desert people and those from the mountain clans, all laughing and chatting as they waited for the Trials to begin.

Street vendors weaved between the rows, selling roasted nuts and candied fruit, while in the main arena a band played a raucous song about the brave Masters of the Beasts of the past.

"I wasn't sure about all this pomp and ceremony," Elenna said, leaning in close to Tom. "But I have to admit, Rotu's done a great job!"

After a series of Beast attacks on Tangala, Queen Aroha had asked her nephew Prince Rotu to find two new heroes to protect the kingdom. Tom and Elenna had been drafted in to select the candidates, while the prince focussed on his own area of expertise: the entertainment.

"It's good to see the people enjoying themselves after everything that's happened," Tom said.

"And Aroha's definitely made the

right choice!" Daltec added. "You and Elenna can't be in two places at once, which means Tangala definitely needs its own Master of the Beasts!"

A gong sounded from the far side of the arena where Prince Rotu sat on a raised dais, his gold-and-silver dress armour gleaming in the sun. He lifted a hand and the music faded, an expectant hush falling over the crowd.

"Let the first contestants come forward!" Rotu cried.

Four participants – all younger than Tom – hurried from their fenced enclosure and into the main arena. *I hope they all do well!* Each walked with their head held high, but their faces were solemn and pinched with nerves as the hopefuls took up their places before the prince.

"I'm glad we never had to do this," Elenna whispered.

"Me too," Tom said. He knew that many of the contestants would never even have set foot in Pania before, let alone been addressed by royalty.

Rotu pointed to the first contender, a tall, lithe girl with choppy dark hair and a serious look in her eyes. "Introduce yourself," he said.

The girl bowed low, then took a massive axe from a belt at her waist. "I am Katya," she said, tossing the axe from hand to hand, as if

it weighed
nothing at all.
"I come from
the Forest
of Shadows.
I pledge my
axe to you,
and to all
of Tangala."

Read
OSSIRON THE FLESHLESS KILLER
to find out what happens next!

Don't miss the thrilling new series from Adam Blade!

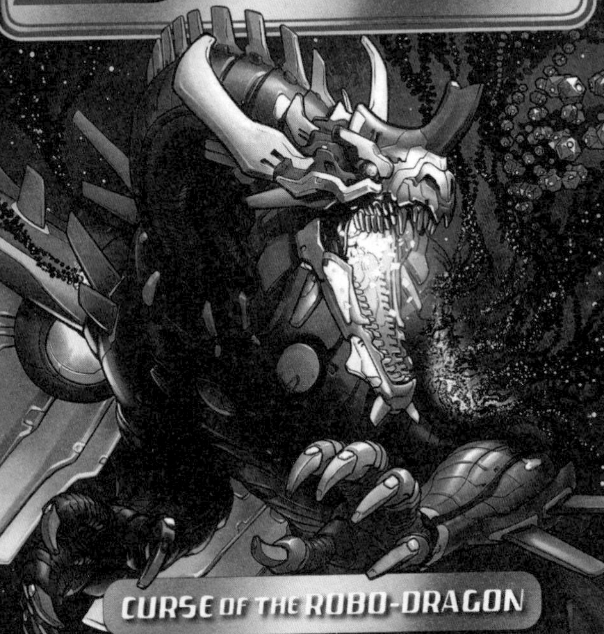